better together*

* This book is best read together, grownup and kid.

a kids
book
about

a kids book about NEURO- DIVERSITY

by Laura Petix, MS OTR/L

A Kids Co.
Editor Emma Wolf
Designer Rick DeLucco
Creative Director Rick DeLucco
Studio Manager Kenya Feldes
Sales Director Melanie Wilkins
Head of Books Jennifer Goldstein
CEO and Founder Jelani Memory

DK
Editor Emma Roberts
Senior Production Editor Jennifer Murray
Senior Production Controller Louise Minihane
Senior Acquisitions Editor Katy Flint
Acquisitions Project Editor Sara Forster
Managing Art Editor Vicky Short
Publishing Director Mark Searle
DK would like to thank Dr Cassie Coleman

First published in Great Britain in 2025 by
Dorling Kindersley Limited
20 Vauxhall Bridge Road,
London SW1V 2SA
A Penguin Random House Company

The authorised representative in the EEA is
Dorling Kindersley Verlag GmbH. Arnulfstr. 124, 80636 Munich, Germany

A CIP catalogue record for this book is available from the British Library.

ISBN: 978-0-2417-2593-1

Printed and bound in China

www.dk.com

akidsco.com

This book was made with Forest
Stewardship Council™ certified
paper – one small step in DK's
commitment to a sustainable future.
Learn more at www.dk.com/uk/
information/sustainability

To Liliana: your brain is beautiful and unique. Don't ever let anyone tell you otherwise.

Thank you for teaching me how to be a better parent. Thank you for being patient with me. Thank you for being you. I love you.

Intro
for grownups

What do you think of when you think of neurodiversity? Maybe you think of a person, or a label, or a diagnosis. Maybe you think of the kid you're sharing this book with. The truth is, the entire human species is neurodiverse. We have different brains from one another, and that's what makes us who we are! Our brains communicate using neurons throughout our body that help us learn, communicate, play, and experience the world in a very specific way.

Some people's brains have wiring that's even more unique than others', and theirs is called a neurodivergent brain. People with neurodivergent brains experience the world differently, which means they learn, communicate, and play differently. This book will help illustrate that neurodivergent brains are not worse than neurotypical brains. In fact, I can't wait to show you just how awesome neurodivergent brains are! Let's go!

What do you know about your brain?

WHAT DOES IT LOOK LIKE ?

WHERE IS IT ?

WHAT DOES IT DO ?

Do you know the answers to these questions?

If not, no worries!
We'll cover a lot of things
about the brain in this book.

**Everything you do
and why you do it is
because of your brain.**

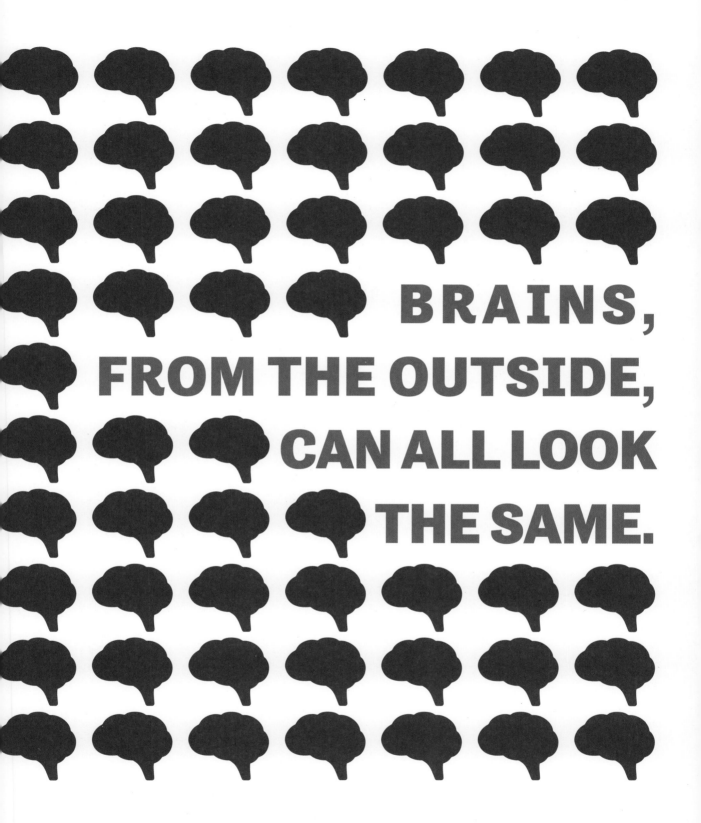

BRAINS, FROM THE OUTSIDE, CAN ALL LOOK THE SAME.

But there are certain parts of the brain that aren't so visible, and those little parts are what make us all different.

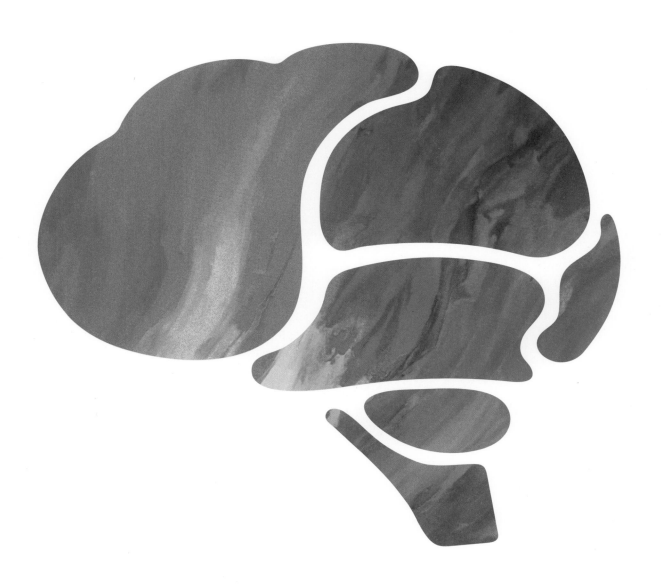

In your brain, there are cells called neurons. And the way these neurons connect in your brain is what makes you who you are.

These connections make you:

feel excited for your birthday,

love the taste of your favourite food,

remember the words to your favourite song, or

really fast when you're playing tag. (Or any other game you're good at!)

So, everyone's brain is different. Everyone's brain learns, plays, communicates, and experiences the world differently.

And that's called

NEURODI

IVERSITY.

To get really specific here, "neuro" means neurons (remember those cells?) and "diversity" means difference.

**Neurodiversity is good!
And it's something to celebrate.**

That's what we're here to do today!

Even though everyone has a different brain, most humans have a similar neurotype*.

The 2 main neurotypes are...

*A type of brain.

neurotypical
and neurodivergent.

For example, most neurotypical brains can learn by sitting still while listening to their teacher.

Or they communicate happiness by smiling, clapping, and saying, "YAY!"

Or they feel comfortable playing hide-and-seek.

Or they want cozy hugs from someone they love!

Neurotypical brains can have differences, too, but they share many similarities.

Neurodivergent brains are distinct because their connections are even more unique.

Instead of sitting still, a person with a neurodivergent brain might learn best by standing, or fidgeting with something.

Instead of clapping, they might communicate happiness by flapping their hands.

Instead of hide-and-seek, they might like making patterns with toys or talking about a favourite show.

Instead of hugs, they might want a high five or no touch at all.

Let's pause and think about how *your* brain works!

WHAT DO YOU NEED IN ORDER TO LEARN ?

WHEN YOU EXPERIENCE FEELINGS, HOW DO YOU LIKE TO SHARE THEM ?

WHAT ARE SOME THINGS THAT MAKE YOUR BODY FEEL CALM ?

Turn to who you're reading with and ask them the same questions.

What did you find out? I bet you noticed some differences between you and the person reading this book with you.

Cool, right?

THAT'S NEURO

DIVERSITY!

Now, I want you to think about your classroom or your neighbourhood.

Do you know someone who expresses their feelings differently to what you're familiar with?

Do they communicate in ways other than using their voice?

Or wear the same thing every day?

Or focus on their hands instead of looking at the person they're talking to?

Have you ever seen someone be very emotional or have a big reaction to something and you didn't understand why?

Some people have brains which experience some things in the world as unsafe, or they just don't feel right.

For example – imagine eating with your family. Your grownups usually make the same meal, but this time they add something different to it.

You might not like the new version of the meal as much, but you still eat it!

But for someone with a neurodivergent brain, this unexpected change might feel really big or scary, and their body responds to that.

And this can look like crying, screaming, or moving their body in big ways.

How does it feel
when you see someone
react differently from you?
Maybe uncomfortable
or confusing?

I've got a little secret for you.

Part of the reason why it feels uncomfortable is because it's different from what neurotypical brains are used to.

The truth is, society is designed for neurotypical brains and behaviours. And this excludes neurodivergent people.

BUT WE CAN CHANGE THAT!

What if, instead of thinking, *That's weird,* **or,** *Why are they acting like that?* **we thought,** *That must feel really hard for them,* **or,** *Hmm, that's a way of doing things that's different from mine!*

If one of your classmates chooses to rock their body or fidget with something in their hands during reading time, that is likely how they learn best.

If you notice someone who wears headphones in the supermarket to limit the sounds around them, don't point or stare.

If you know someone who likes to play the same thing over and over again, ask them questions about what they enjoy and see if you can join them.

So basically, if you see someone whose behaviour looks different to yours in your community, just notice it, and think...

HEY! NEURO-DIVERSITY! THAT'S COOL!

Some things matter more to some brains than other brains.

Some brains have different needs than other brains.

Your brain might need a quiet space to focus on homework, and someone else's brain might need music to focus on homework.

Everyone deserves to feel comfortable being who they are and expressing themselves in a way which is natural to them.

What if someone said you had to wear shoes on your hands every day?

How silly would that feel?

Well, that's how society treats neurodivergent people a lot of the time!

They are expected to laugh at jokes they don't understand, do things with their bodies that don't feel natural, or communicate in ways that feel overwhelming.

This is essentially asking them to change the way their brains work.

Let's not ask neurodivergent people to act more neurotypical.

Let's acknowledge, celebrate, and love the unique wiring of every brain.

And that starts with you!

As soon as you close this book, put your hands on your head and think about all of the wonderful things about your brain that make you, you.

Share them with people you love.

FEEL
THE JOY
IN
ACCEPTANCE.

And then celebrate the neurodiversity around you.

**And how our world
is better for it.**

Outro
for grownups

You did it! By reading this book with your kid, you helped make the world a more neurodiversity-affirming place. But your work doesn't end here. Please keep this conversation alive in your house, your classroom, and your community by truly celebrating the differences you notice and leaving space for people to be who they are, in a way that honours the way their brains are wired.

Mindset shifts are the best place to start. For example, if you overhear someone saying, "That's weird! Why do they talk like that?" you might help them rephrase by saying, "Hmm, they communicate differently than we do. That's new." You could help your kid notice their own neurodiversity by saying, "Wow! Your brain needs extra movement when you're doing maths."

Instead of placing the responsibility on neurodivergent individuals to conform to neurotypical norms, let's work towards a society that is more inclusive, more flexible, and more able to make space for neurodivergent people to exist just as they are, right alongside neurotypical people.

About The Author

As an occupational therapist, Laura (she/her) works with families to help them better understand and support neurodivergent brains, without focusing on making them appear more neurotypical. Laura is neurodivergent, with a brain wired for anxiety and sensory sensitivity, much like her daughter. This experience combined with a clinical background in studying how the brain works has informed Laura's skilled approach to explaining these concepts to families and kids.

Initially, Laura focused on teaching grownups about neurodiversity and how a kid's behaviour is directly impacted by their nervous system and sensory processing abilities. But she realized that kids need this information too. Neurodivergent individuals can be proud of their brains, and not ashamed because of their behaviour. And neurotypical kids need to be aware that different brains exist, and we can love and respect them just as they are.

 @Theotbutterfly   The Sensory W.I.S.E. Solutions podcast

Made to empower.

a kids book about racism
by Jelani Memory

a kids book about ANXIETY
by Ross Szabo

a kids book about DISABILITY
by Kristine Napper

a kids book about IMAGINATION
by LEVAR BURTON

a kids book about belonging
by Kevin Carroll

a kids book about failure
by Dr Laymon Hicks

a kids book about GRATITUDE
by Ben Kenyon

a kids book about LIFE ONLINE
by Dave S. Anderson & Blake Fleischacker

a kids book about body image
by Rebecca Alexander

a kids book about IMMIGRATION
by MJ Calderon

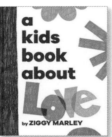
a kids book about EMPATHY
by Daron K. Roberts

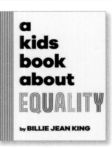
a kids book about GENDER
by Dale Mueller

a kids book about Love
by ZIGGY MARLEY

a kids book about EQUALITY
by BILLIE JEAN KING

a kids book about MONEY
by Adam Stramwasser

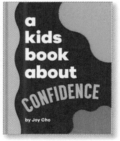
a kids book about FEMINISM
by Emma McIlroy

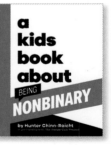
a kids book about adventure
by Dr Ben Tertin

a kids book about CLIMATE CHANGE
by Zanagee Artis & Olivia Greenspan

a kids book about CONFIDENCE
by Joy Cho

a kids book about BEING NONBINARY
by Hunter Chinn-Raicht

Discover more at akidsco.com